Hans Christian Andersen
The TINDERBOX
Illustrated by James Warhola

RETOLD BY PEGGY THOMSON

Simon & Schuster Books for Young Readers

Published by Simon & Schuster
New York • London • Toronto • Sydney • Tokyo • Singapore

SIMON & SCHUSTER BOOKS FOR YOUNG READERS
Simon & Schuster Building, Rockefeller Center,
1230 Avenue of the Americas, New York, New York 10020.
Text copyright © 1991 by Peggy Thomson
Illustrations copyright © 1991 by James Warhola
SIMON & SCHUSTER BOOKS FOR YOUNG READERS
is a trademark of Simon & Schuster

Designed by Lucille Chomowicz
The text of this book is set in Cloister.
The illustrations were done in watercolor.
Manufactured in Singapore 10 9 8 7 6 5 4 3 2 1

Library of Congress Cataloging-in-Publication Data. Thomson, Peggy. Hans
Christian Andersen's The tinderbox/retold by Peggy Thomson, illustrated by
James Warhola. Summary: A retelling of Andersen's classic tale of a brave
soldier who finds love and fortune in a magic tinderbox. [1. Fairy tales.]
I. Warhola, James, ill.   II. Andersen, H. C. (Hans Christian), 1805-1875.
Fyrtøjet. English. III. Title.   IV. Title: Tinderbox.   PZ8.T3767Han
1991 [Fic]—dc20   89-48014   ISBN 0-671-70546-6

To Zonker Harris III — JW

To the memory of my father — PT

One day, a soldier went marching down the road on his way home from war. He was a handsome, brave fellow who had fought many battles and risked much, and he was glad to be returning home. The soldier was weary and hungry; but even in his weariness, he stood up straight and marched evenly, with a heavy pack on his back and a shining sword by his side.

Suddenly, an old witch appeared on the path. She was ugly to look at, with warts covering her wrinkled face, a crooked nose, and a chin so long that it jiggled as she spoke.

"Good day, soldier!" she cackled, and her smile revealed crooked teeth and a bright red tongue.

"Good day, old woman!" replied the soldier.

"I see you've been to war. Would you do an old woman a favor? There is a great reward in it for you."

The soldier looked down at his worn boots and faded clothes and felt his empty stomach growling. He thought how nice it would be to have some money for food.

"What would you like me to do?" he asked.

The old witch smiled and pointed to a huge old oak tree with gnarled branches.

"That tree is hollow inside. If you climb all the way to the top of the trunk, you can slide down to a passage at the bottom. Don't worry about getting out again; I'll tie this rope around your waist to pull you out when you're ready."

"What should I do down there?" asked the soldier.

"Oh, there is money in there," replied the witch, hissing. "Much money." She smiled her crooked smile. "When you reach the bottom, you will find yourself in a passage with three doors leading to different rooms. In the first room is a large chest, with a big dog seated on top. His eyes are as round as saucers, but don't be afraid. Spread this apron on the ground and lift him onto it. After you have done that, you can help yourself to as much money as you desire.

"It is all copper, but if you desire silver, go into the next room. That one has a dog with eyes as large as wagon wheels; but he won't harm you, either, if you spread out the apron and place him on it. If you prefer gold, you will find it in the third room. The dog guarding that chest has eyes as large as the moon, but all you have to do is put him on the apron and the gold is yours."

"That sounds easy, old woman," the soldier said. "But what do you want?"

"Not a thing," said the old witch. "I just ask that you bring me the old tinderbox that my grandmother left there."

After all he had been through, it seemed like an easy task to the soldier, so he let the witch tie the rope around his waist. Then he carefully climbed up the tree, slid down inside the trunk, and found himself in a large hallway, just as the witch had said.

The first door he saw was painted bright red; and when he pushed it open, he saw a large dog seated on a chest, staring at him with huge, round eyes. The soldier was a little afraid, but he did as the old witch had instructed. After the dog was on the apron, he filled his pockets with copper.

The next door in the passage was bright yellow; and when the soldier entered the room, he saw another dog, with eyes as large as wagon wheels. This one was even more fearsome, but he put him on the apron, filled his bulging pockets with silver, and went on to the third door.

This door was bright green; and when he pushed it open, the soldier gasped. Seated with his paws on the chest in the middle of the floor was a dog with eyes as large as a full moon. But again the soldier remembered the instructions, put the dog on the apron, and opened the chest.

His eyes widened. There was enough gold for a king! He emptied his pockets of the copper and silver pieces, and filled his pockets, his knapsack, and his cap full of gold. "Now I shall live well," he thought.

The soldier hurried back to the opening of the passage, delighted with his good fortune. But just as he was about to call up to the old witch, he remembered the tinderbox and went back to fetch it.

"All right, old woman," he called after he had found it. The witch pulled him back up; and as soon as he was on solid ground again, he asked, "What did you want the tinderbox for?"

"That's my very own secret," the old witch hissed, smiling craftily. "You have your money. Now give me the box."

But the soldier was feeling greedy. He had more gold in his pockets than he had ever owned in his life. But he thought to himself, "Perhaps there is something even more valuable in the tinderbox or she wouldn't want it so badly. Maybe I should hold on to it!"

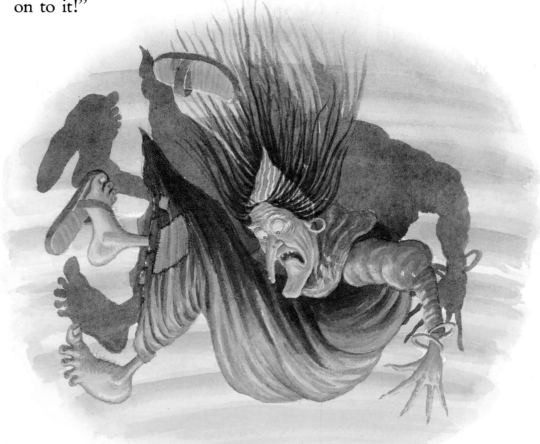

Without thinking twice, he hoisted the old witch over his shoulder, staggered back up the tree, and dropped her into the hollow trunk. She was very old and very heavy, and the walls of the passage were very high and smooth. Calling out to the soldier, she cursed him for his greed, but she was utterly helpless. To this day she is trapped in the hollow tree with chests full of coins and only the echo of her own voice.

As for the soldier, he marched into the nearest town, feeling wealthy and clever, outfitted himself with a new suit of clothes, and enjoyed a fine supper. By nightfall, he had found lodging for himself.

For the next few months, the soldier led a life of luxury, enjoying good food, entertaining guests every night with lavish parties, and traveling whenever he wished. But he gave money to the poor whenever they asked, for he remembered only too well how it was to be hungry.

The gold did not last forever, though, and after months of such extravagance, the soldier found himself with only five cents in his pocket. He was so poor that he did not even have enough money to buy a candle. One evening, as it grew dark, he remembered the tinderbox from the hollow tree. He pulled it out from under his mattress and struck the flint for fire. But no sooner did the sparks fly out than the dog with huge, saucer eyes appeared before him.

"What do you wish, Master?"

"What a treasure!" the soldier thought as he stared at the old tinderbox. He looked up at the fearsome dog and said, "Money—bring me money so that I may be wealthy again."

The dog was back within an hour with a bag full of copper coins.

The soldier tried the tinderbox out again and realized how valuable it was. Strike it once and the dog from the chest of copper coins appeared. Strike it twice and the dog from the chest of silver appeared. But three strikes and the dog with eyes as round as the moon appeared, bearing gold.

The soldier welcomed his good fortune, but soon he grew tired of entertaining and buying fine clothes. There was one thing he desired more than anything else, but all the gold in the world could not buy it for him: He wanted to get a glimpse of the King's daughter. She was rumored to be beautiful, but she was kept in a tall copper castle, because the King had been told by a seer that she would one day marry a common soldier, and he could not bear the thought.

The next time he struck the flint and the dog appeared, saying, "What do you wish, Master?" the soldier replied, "I want to see the famous Princess!"

The dog was out in a flash, and within minutes he returned with the sleeping Princess on his back. The soldier gasped at her beauty and determined at that instant to marry her. The dog ran back to the castle with the Princess still asleep on his back, and the Princess told the King and Queen of the curious dream she had had that night, about riding on a dog's back and being kissed by a soldier.

The King and Queen thought it a silly tale but the Princess's lady-in-waiting was suspicious; and the following night, when the soldier again summoned the dog to fetch the Princess, the lady-in-waiting followed them, running as fast as her legs could carry her. When the dog raced into the soldier's house, the lady-in-waiting quickly drew a large X on the door.

The very next day, the King and Queen and the court officials went to look.

"Here is the place," cried the Queen triumphantly, pointing to a large white X on a door.

"No, my dear, *this* is the place," said the King, pointing to another X mark.

But they were both wrong—because *every single* door in town now had an X chalked on it. The clever dog had noticed it on his way back, and he had marked every door to throw them off the track.

But the Queen was also clever. That night, she made a tiny little bag of silk and filled it with rice. Then she tied it to the Princess's dress and cut a small hole in the bottom. Later, as the Princess was again carried to the soldier's house, the rice left a trail all the way from the castle.

Before he knew what had happened, the soldier was seized and thrown into the dungeon. He was destined to be hanged.

The poor soldier had nothing now, not even his tinderbox, which he had left at home. One day as he stared sadly out the one tiny window in the dungeon, he spotted a young beggar boy and called out to him, "You there! Wait a minute! If you'd like to earn some pennies for yourself, do a favor for a poor prisoner. If you'll run to my house and fetch my tinderbox for me, I'll reward you handsomely, I promise."

In a flash, the boy was back with the tinderbox—and not a minute too soon.

The gallows had already been set up for the soldier, and a curious crowd had gathered for the spectacle. The soldier was led out to his punishment; but as he mounted the steps to the scaffold, he had a brilliant thought.

"Majesty, please allow me
one last pipe before I die," he
asked the King. The King could
hardly refuse such a request, so the
soldier took out his tinderbox and
struck it once, twice, three times; and
soon the astonished crowd saw three dogs
appear, all with large, round, staring eyes.

"Save me!" cried the soldier, not wasting any time.

Quick as a flash, the largest dog, with eyes as round and
bright as the moon, opened his wide jaws and gobbled up the
King and Queen, swallowing them whole.

From the depths of the dog's stomach, the people could hear them calling to the soldier. "Let us out! Help! Save me! Let us out and you shall have all the gold you desire!"

"I don't want any more gold," said the soldier, remembering how he had gotten into trouble in the first place. "But I do have one request; and if you grant it, your lives will be spared. Let me have the Princess as my wife. I love her dearly, and I will treat her well."

The King and Queen could hardly refuse, and besides, the soldier seemed like a decent fellow.

"So be it," said the King; and, quick as a flash, the huge dog stretched his jaws, barked loudly, and out of his enormous mouth popped the astonished King and Queen.

When the King saw how lovingly the soldier regarded his daughter and how lovingly she returned his gaze, he saw that he had been wrong to keep her hidden away for so long. He arranged for a lavish wedding, and the soldier and the Princess were given a fine palace to make their home.

The rooms were spacious and bright, there was a well-tended garden in the back, and the front door was carefully guarded by three huge dogs with round, staring eyes.